D1159708

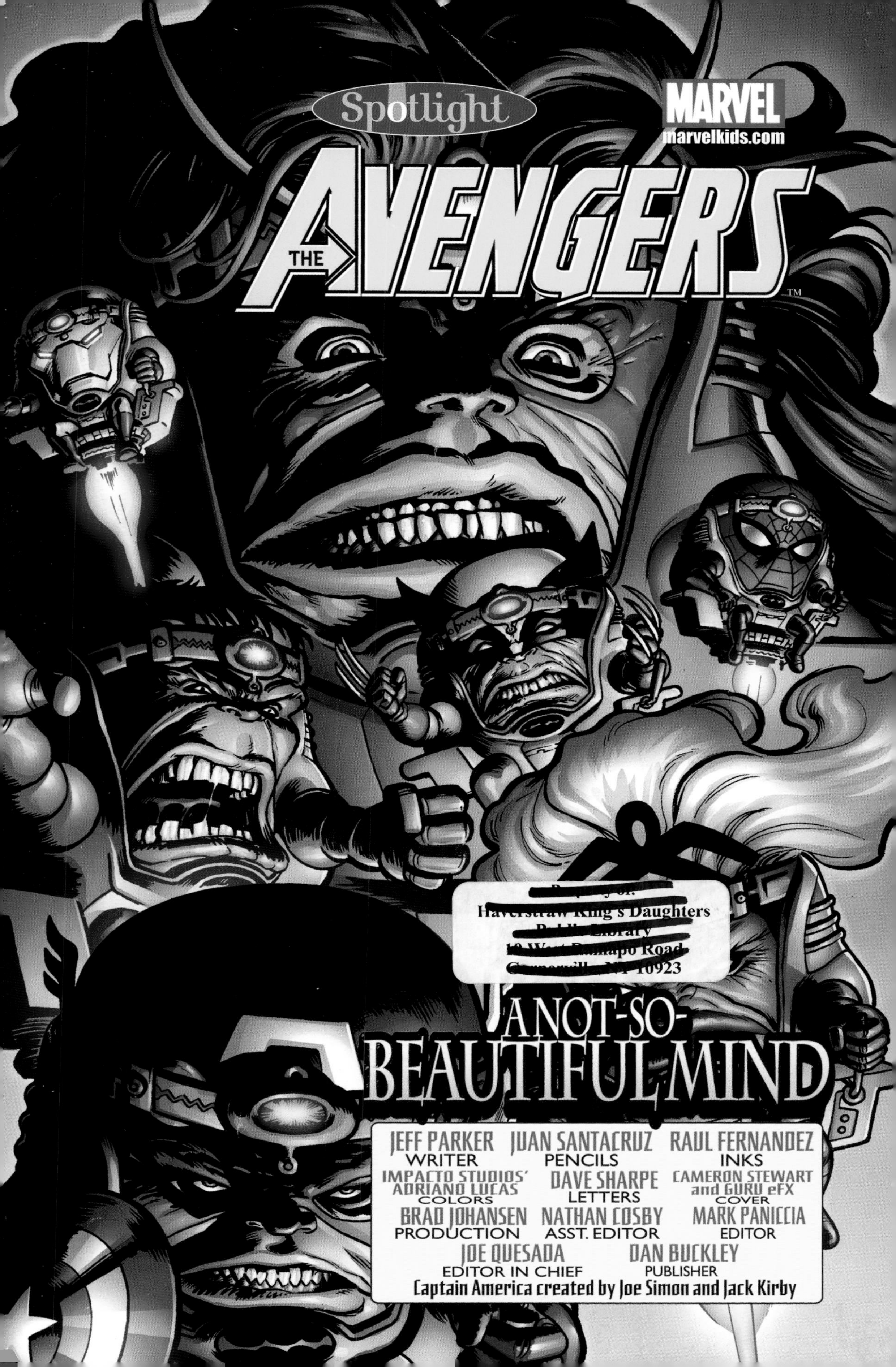
Spotlight
MARVEL
marvelkids.com
THE AVENGERS™
A NOT-SO-BEAUTIFUL MIND
JEFF PARKER WRITER
JUAN SANTACRUZ PENCILS
RAUL FERNANDEZ INKS
IMPACTO STUDIOS' ADRIANO LUCAS COLORS
DAVE SHARPE LETTERS
CAMERON STEWART and GURU eFX COVER
BRAD JOHANSEN PRODUCTION
NATHAN COSBY ASST. EDITOR
MARK PANICCIA EDITOR
JOE QUESADA EDITOR IN CHIEF
DAN BUCKLEY PUBLISHER
Captain America created by Joe Simon and Jack Kirby

visit us at www.abdopublishing.com

Reinforced library bound edition published in 2013 by Spotlight, a division of the ABDO Group, 8000 West 78th Street, Edina, Minnesota 55439. Spotlight produces high-quality reinforced library bound editions for schools and libraries. Published by agreement with Marvel Entertainment, LLC. The stories, characters, and incidents mentioned are entirely fictional. All rights reserved. Used under authorization.

Printed in the United States of America, North Mankato, Minnesota.
052012
092012
♻ This book contains at least 10% recycled materials.

marvelkids.com

TM & © 2012 Marvel & Subs.

Library of Congress Cataloging-in-Publication Data

Parker, Jeff, 1966-
  A not-so-beautiful mind / story by Jeff Parker ; art by Juan Santacruz. -- Reinforced library bound ed.
      p. cm. -- (Avengers)
  "Marvel."
  Summary: The Avengers fall into the clutches of Modoc, a scientist with a brain of the greatest mass humanly possible.
  ISBN 978-1-61479-017-4 (alk. paper)
  1. Graphic novels. [1. Graphic novels. 2. Superheroes--Fiction. 3. Brain--Fiction.] I. Santacruz, Juan, ill. II. Title.
  PZ7.7.P252Not 2012
  741.5'973--dc23

                              2012000930

ISBN 978-1-61479-017-4 (reinforced library edition)

All Spotlight books are reinforced library binding
and manufactured in the United States of America.

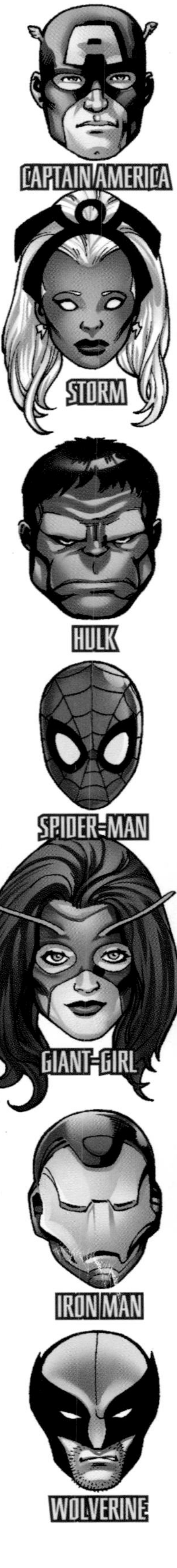

CAPTAIN AMERICA
STORM
HULK
SPIDER-MAN
GIANT-GIRL
IRON MAN
WOLVERINE

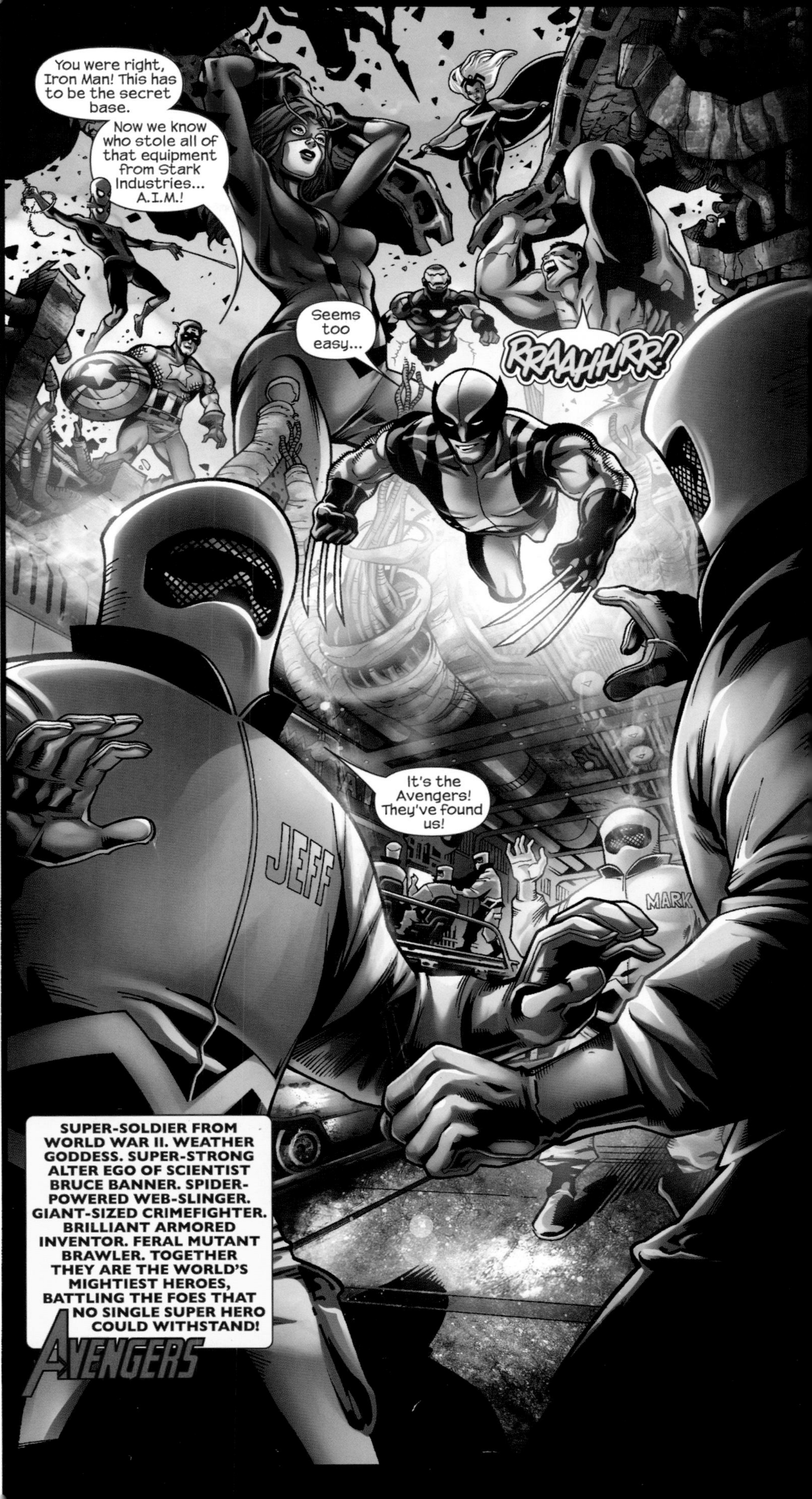

You were right, Iron Man! This has to be the secret base.
Now we know who stole all of that equipment from Stark Industries... A.I.M.!
Seems too easy...
RRAAHHRR!
It's the Avengers! They've found us!
JEFF
MARK
SUPER-SOLDIER FROM WORLD WAR II. WEATHER GODDESS. SUPER-STRONG ALTER EGO OF SCIENTIST BRUCE BANNER. SPIDER-POWERED WEB-SLINGER. GIANT-SIZED CRIMEFIGHTER. BRILLIANT ARMORED INVENTOR. FERAL MUTANT BRAWLER. TOGETHER THEY ARE THE WORLD'S MIGHTIEST HEROES, BATTLING THE FOES THAT NO SINGLE SUPER HERO COULD WITHSTAND!
AVENGERS

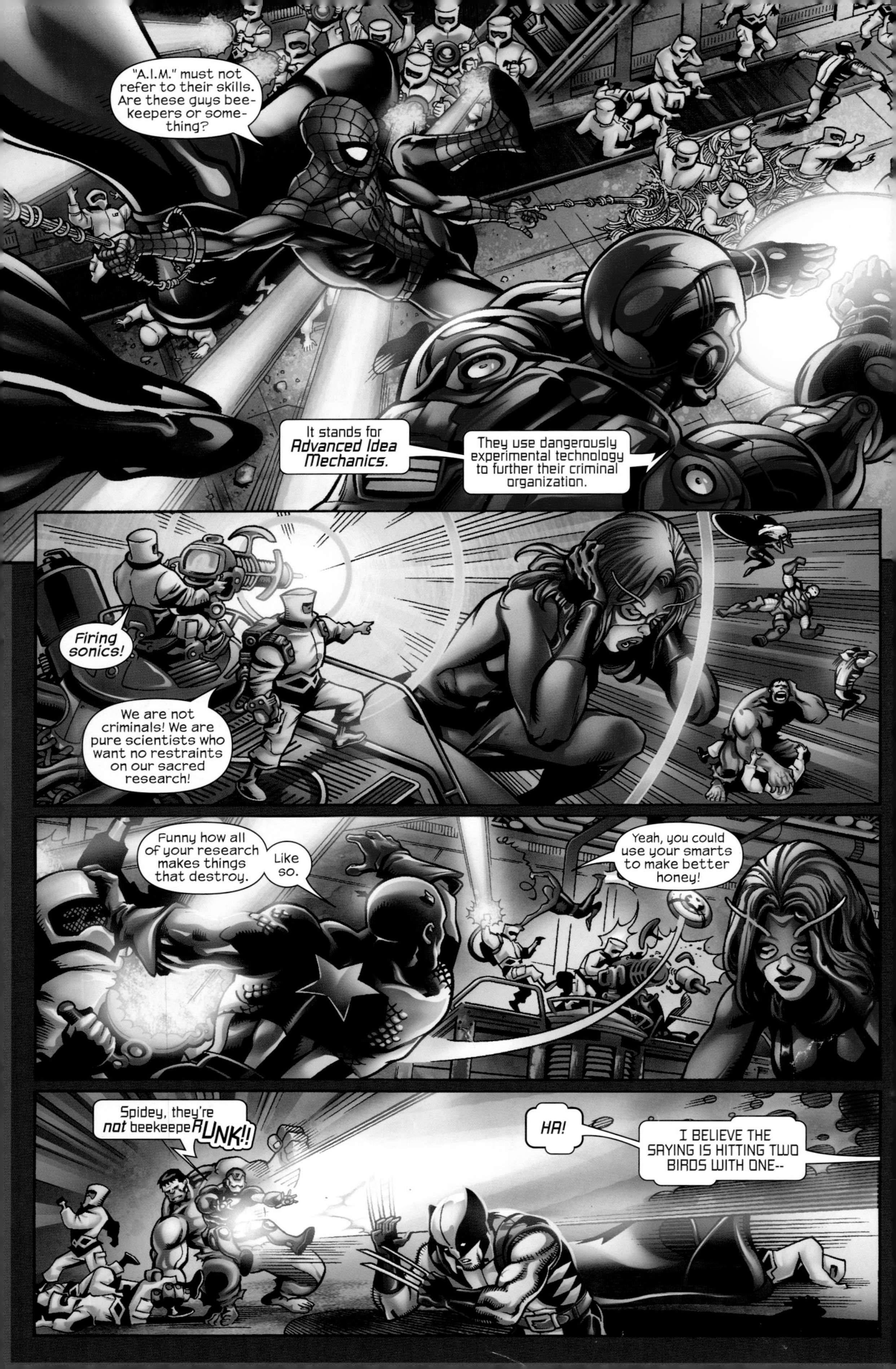

"A.I.M." must not refer to their skills. Are these guys bee-keepers or some-thing?
It stands for *Advanced Idea Mechanics.*
They use dangerously experimental technology to further their criminal organization.
Firing sonics!
We are not criminals! We are pure scientists who want no restraints on our sacred research!
Funny how all of your research makes things that destroy.
Like so.
Yeah, you could use your smarts to make better honey!
Spidey, they're *not* beekeepeRUNK!!
HA!
I BELIEVE THE SAYING IS HITTING TWO BIRDS WITH ONE--

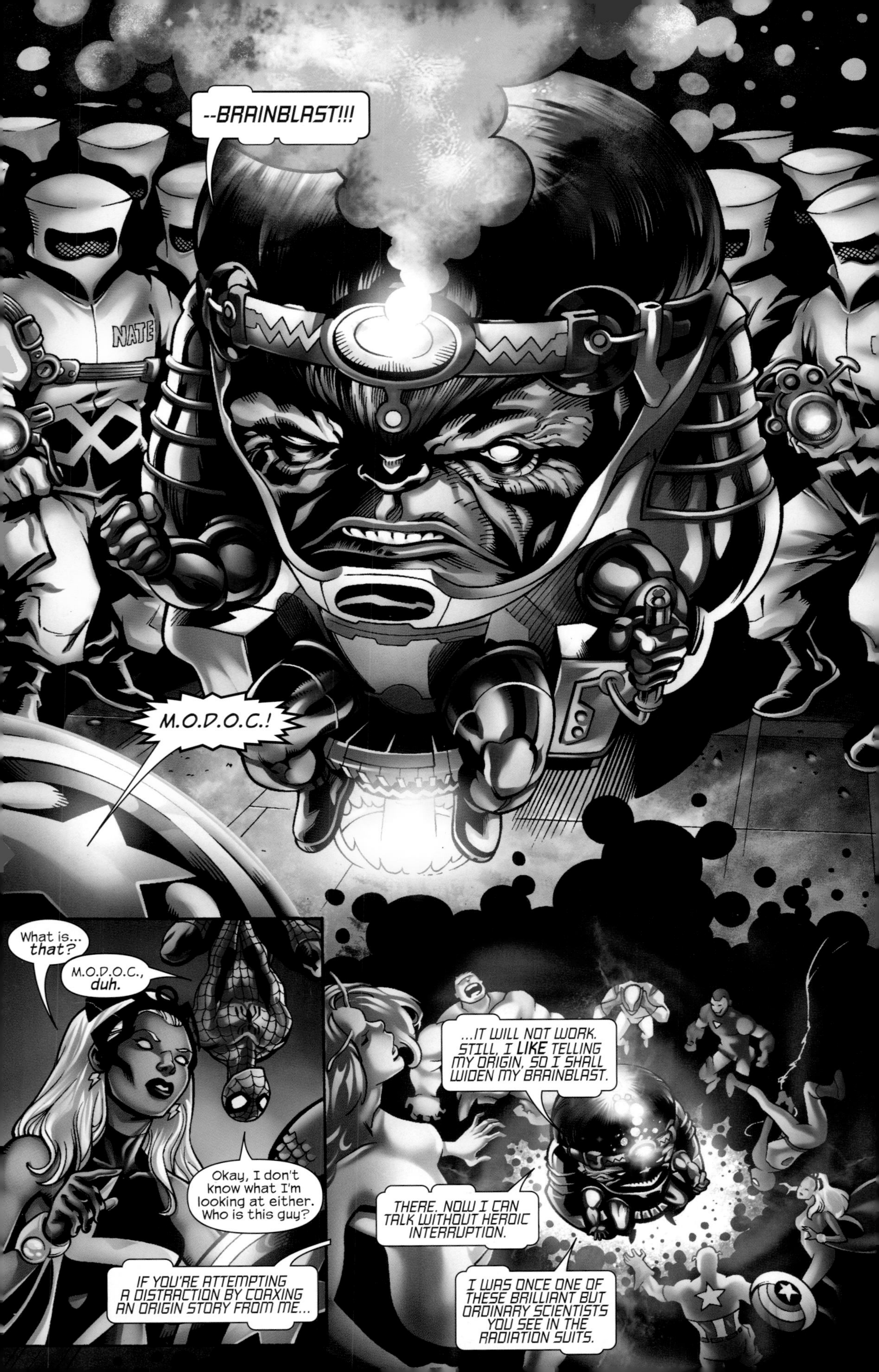

--BRAINBLAST!!!
NATE
M.O.D.O.C.!
What is... that?
M.O.D.O.C., duh.
Okay, I don't know what I'm looking at either. Who is this guy?
IF YOU'RE ATTEMPTING A DISTRACTION BY COAXING AN ORIGIN STORY FROM ME...
...IT WILL NOT WORK. STILL, I LIKE TELLING MY ORIGIN, SO I SHALL WIDEN MY BRAINBLAST.
THERE. NOW I CAN TALK WITHOUT HEROIC INTERRUPTION.
I WAS ONCE ONE OF THESE BRILLIANT BUT ORDINARY SCIENTISTS YOU SEE IN THE RADIATION SUITS.

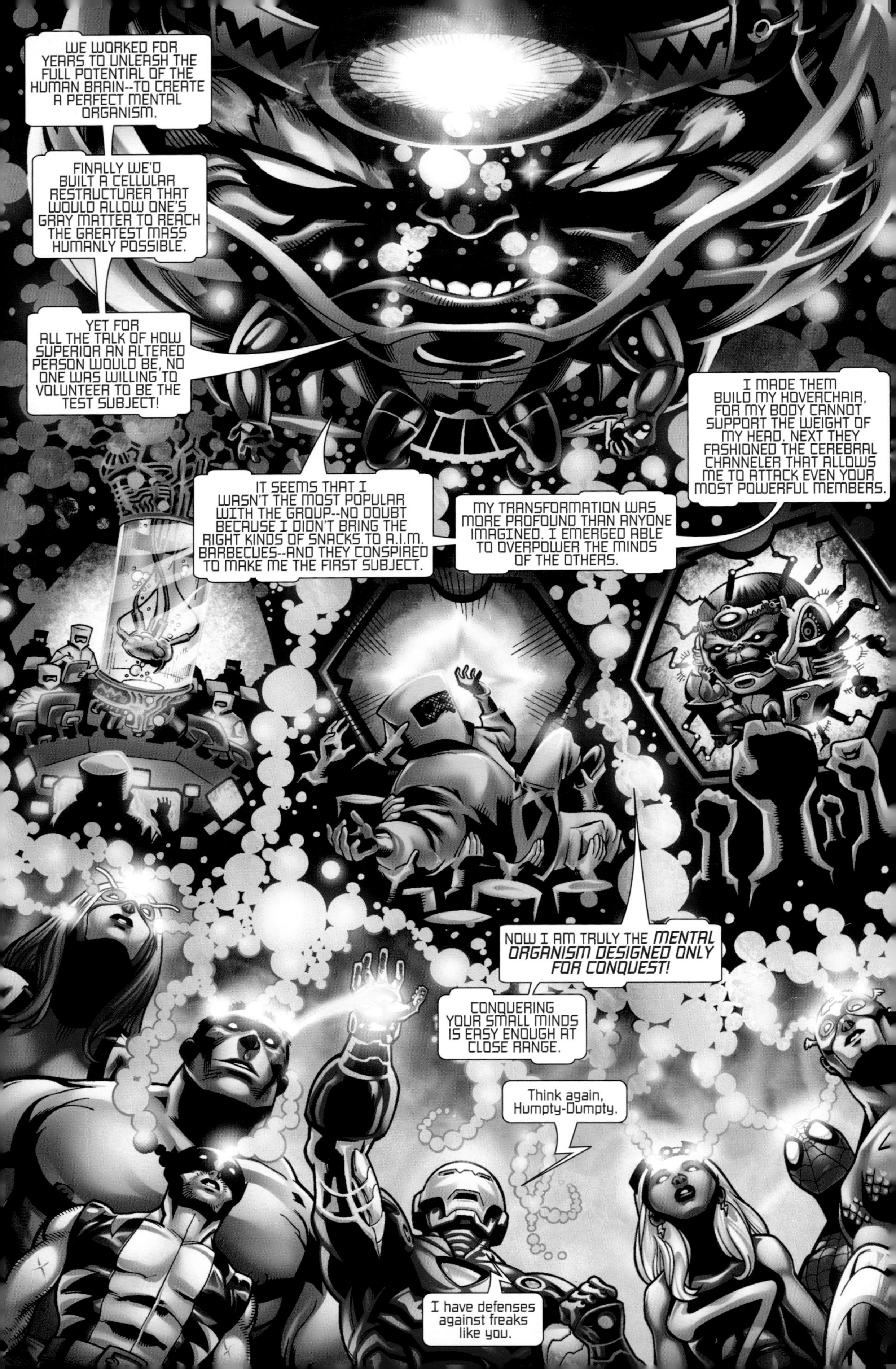
WE WORKED FOR YEARS TO UNLEASH THE FULL POTENTIAL OF THE HUMAN BRAIN--TO CREATE A PERFECT MENTAL ORGANISM.
FINALLY WE'D BUILT A CELLULAR RESTRUCTURER THAT WOULD ALLOW ONE'S GRAY MATTER TO REACH THE GREATEST MASS HUMANLY POSSIBLE.
YET FOR ALL THE TALK OF HOW SUPERIOR AN ALTERED PERSON WOULD BE, NO ONE WAS WILLING TO VOLUNTEER TO BE THE TEST SUBJECT!
IT SEEMS THAT I WASN'T THE MOST POPULAR WITH THE GROUP--NO DOUBT BECAUSE I DIDN'T BRING THE RIGHT KINDS OF SNACKS TO R.I.M. BARBECUES--AND THEY CONSPIRED TO MAKE ME THE FIRST SUBJECT.
MY TRANSFORMATION WAS MORE PROFOUND THAN ANYONE IMAGINED. I EMERGED ABLE TO OVERPOWER THE MINDS OF THE OTHERS.
I MADE THEM BUILD MY HOVERCHAIR, FOR MY BODY CANNOT SUPPORT THE WEIGHT OF MY HEAD. NEXT THEY FASHIONED THE CEREBRAL CHANNELER THAT ALLOWS ME TO ATTACK EVEN YOUR MOST POWERFUL MEMBERS.
NOW I AM TRULY THE *MENTAL ORGANISM DESIGNED ONLY FOR CONQUEST!*
CONQUERING YOUR SMALL MINDS IS EASY ENOUGH AT CLOSE RANGE.
Think again, Humpty-Dumpty.
I have defenses against freaks like you.

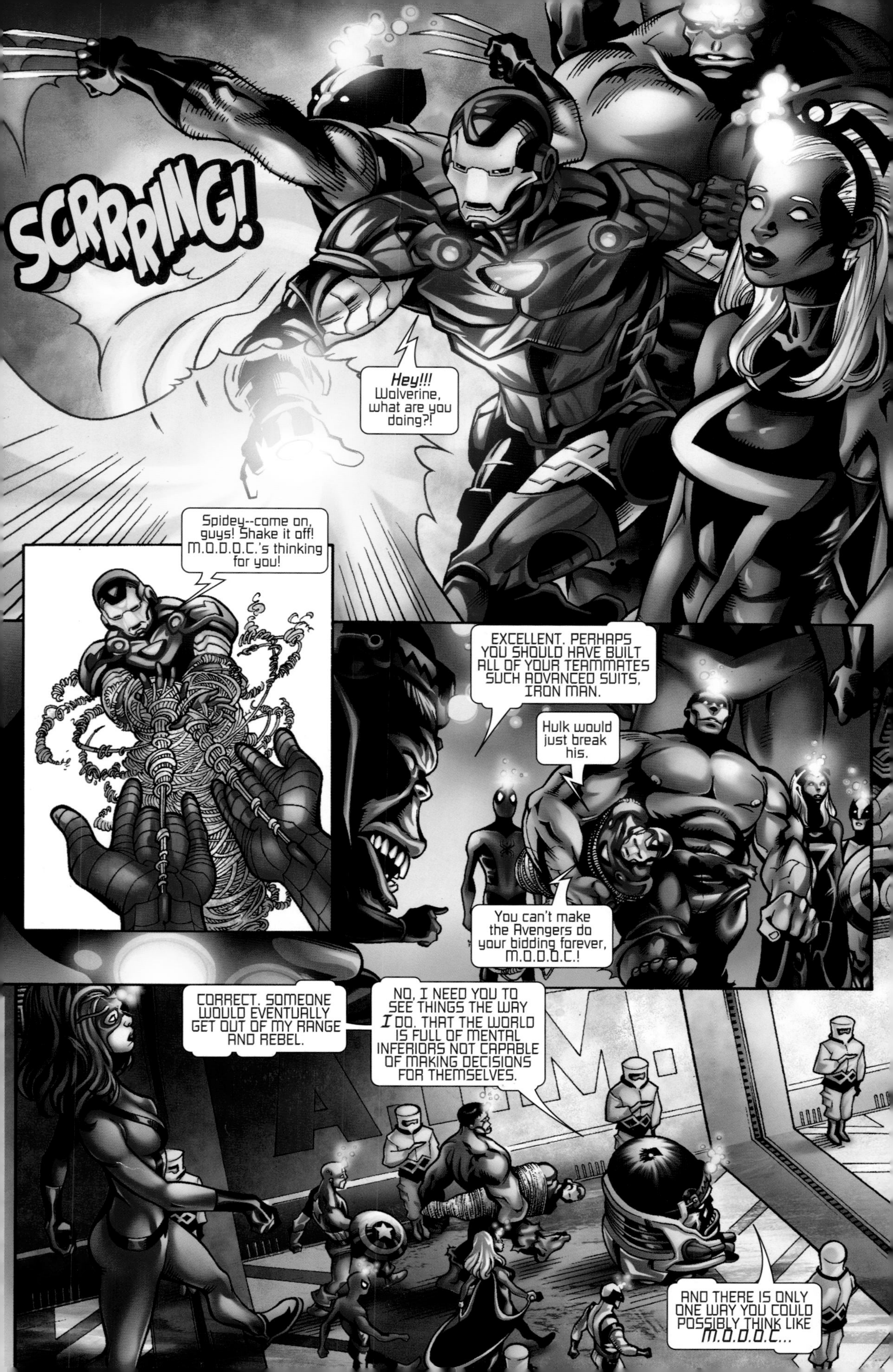
SCRRRING!
Hey!!! Wolverine, what are you doing?!
Spidey--come on, guys! Shake it off! M.O.D.O.C.'s thinking for you!
EXCELLENT. PERHAPS YOU SHOULD HAVE BUILT ALL OF YOUR TEAMMATES SUCH ADVANCED SUITS, IRON MAN.
Hulk would just break his.
You can't make the Avengers do your bidding forever, M.O.D.O.C.!
CORRECT. SOMEONE WOULD EVENTUALLY GET OUT OF MY RANGE AND REBEL.
NO, I NEED YOU TO SEE THINGS THE WAY I DO. THAT THE WORLD IS FULL OF MENTAL INFERIORS NOT CAPABLE OF MAKING DECISIONS FOR THEMSELVES.
AND THERE IS ONLY ONE WAY YOU COULD POSSIBLY THINK LIKE M.O.D.O.C...

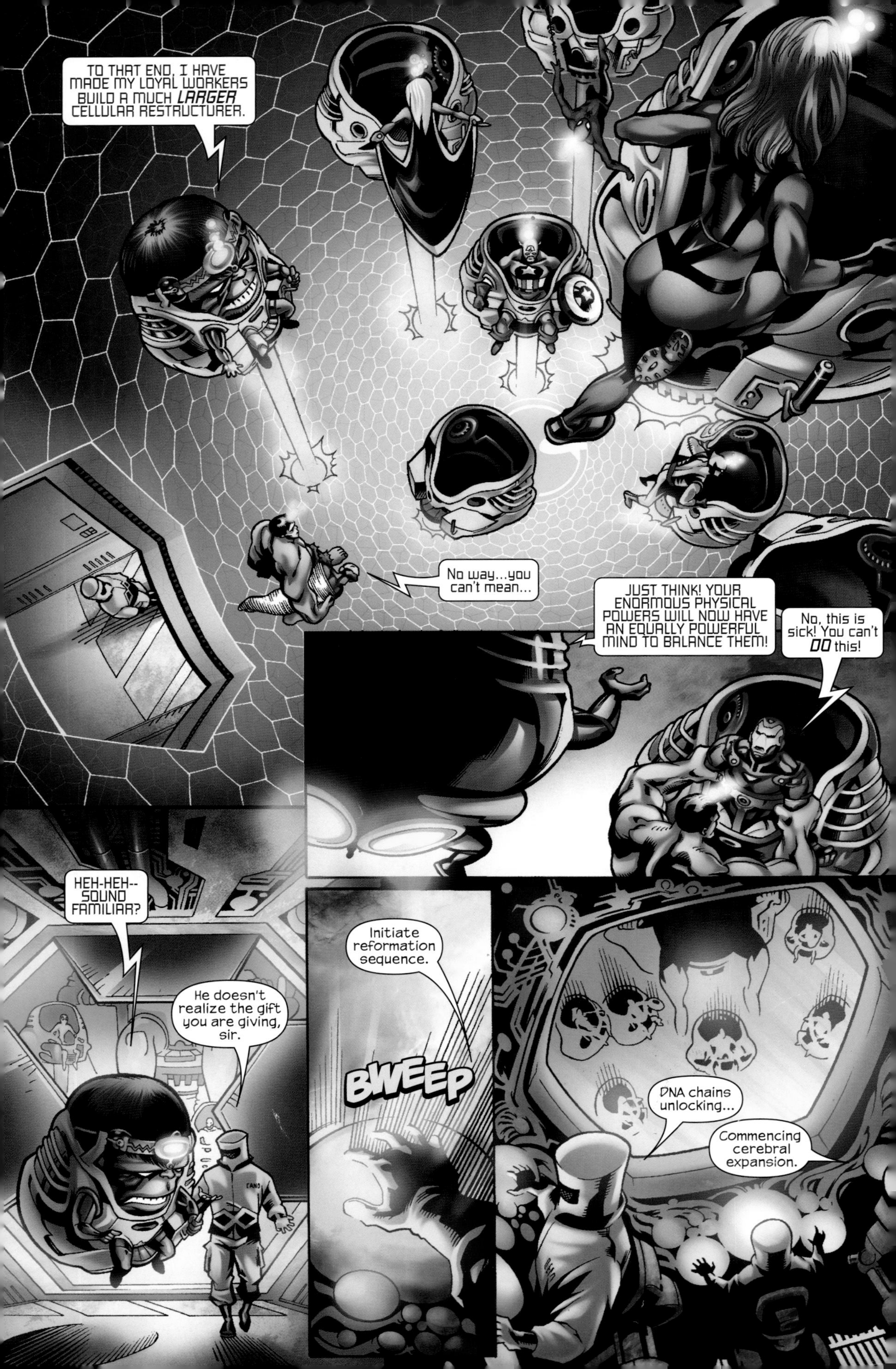
TO THAT END, I HAVE MADE MY LOYAL WORKERS BUILD A MUCH LARGER CELLULAR RESTRUCTURER.
No way...you can't mean...
JUST THINK! YOUR ENORMOUS PHYSICAL POWERS WILL NOW HAVE AN EQUALLY POWERFUL MIND TO BALANCE THEM!
No, this is sick! You can't DO this!
HEH-HEH--SOUND FAMILIAR?
He doesn't realize the gift you are giving, sir.
Initiate reformation sequence.
BWEEP
DNA chains unlocking...
Commencing cerebral expansion.

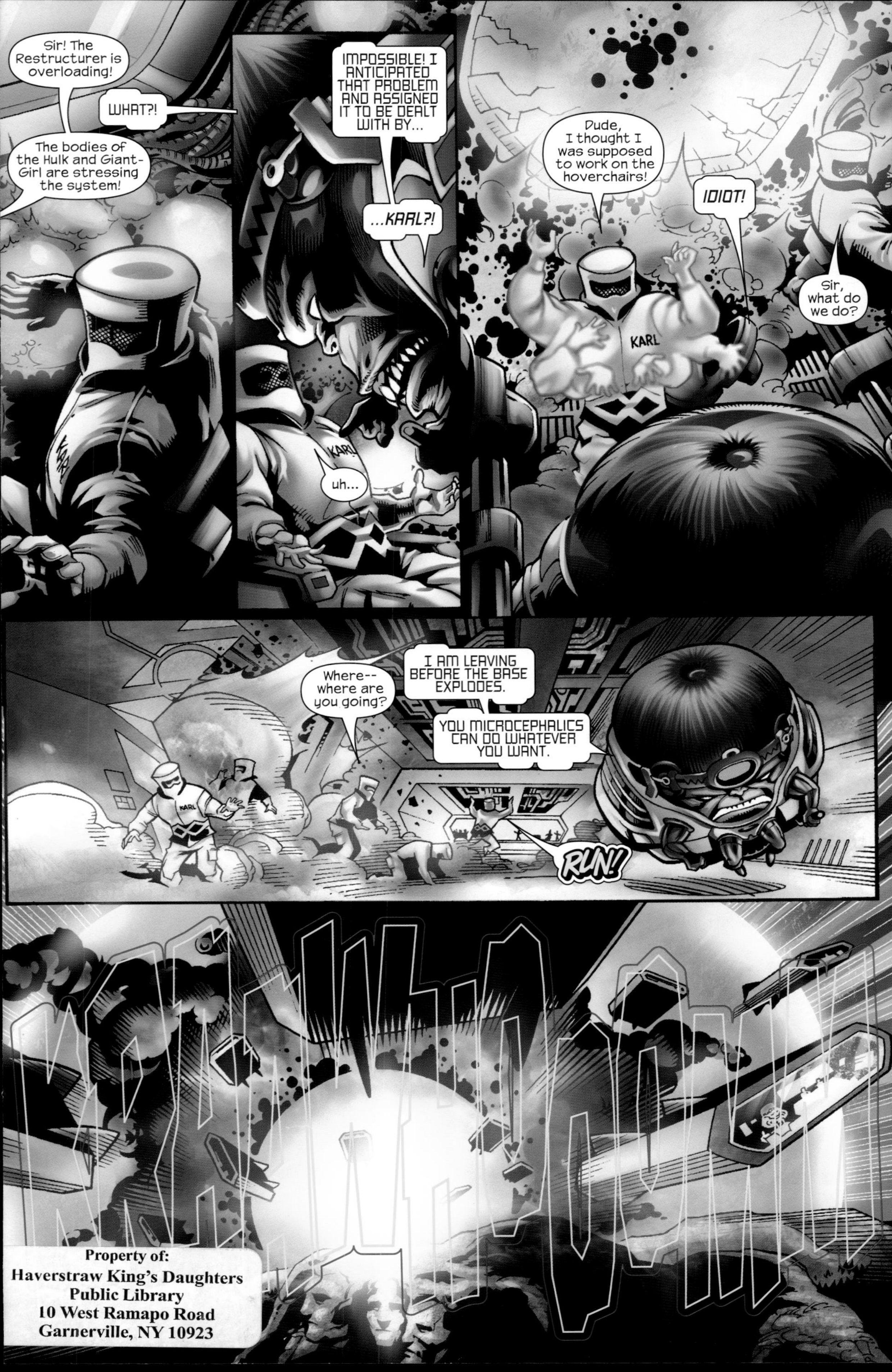
Sir! The Restructurer is overloading!
WHAT?!
The bodies of the Hulk and Giant-Girl are stressing the system!
IMPOSSIBLE! I ANTICIPATED THAT PROBLEM AND ASSIGNED IT TO BE DEALT WITH BY...
...KARL?!
KARL
uh...
Dude, I thought I was supposed to work on the hoverchairs!
IDIOT!
KARL
Sir, what do we do?
Where-- where are you going?
I AM LEAVING BEFORE THE BASE EXPLODES.
YOU MICROCEPHALICS CAN DO WHATEVER YOU WANT.
KARL
RUN!

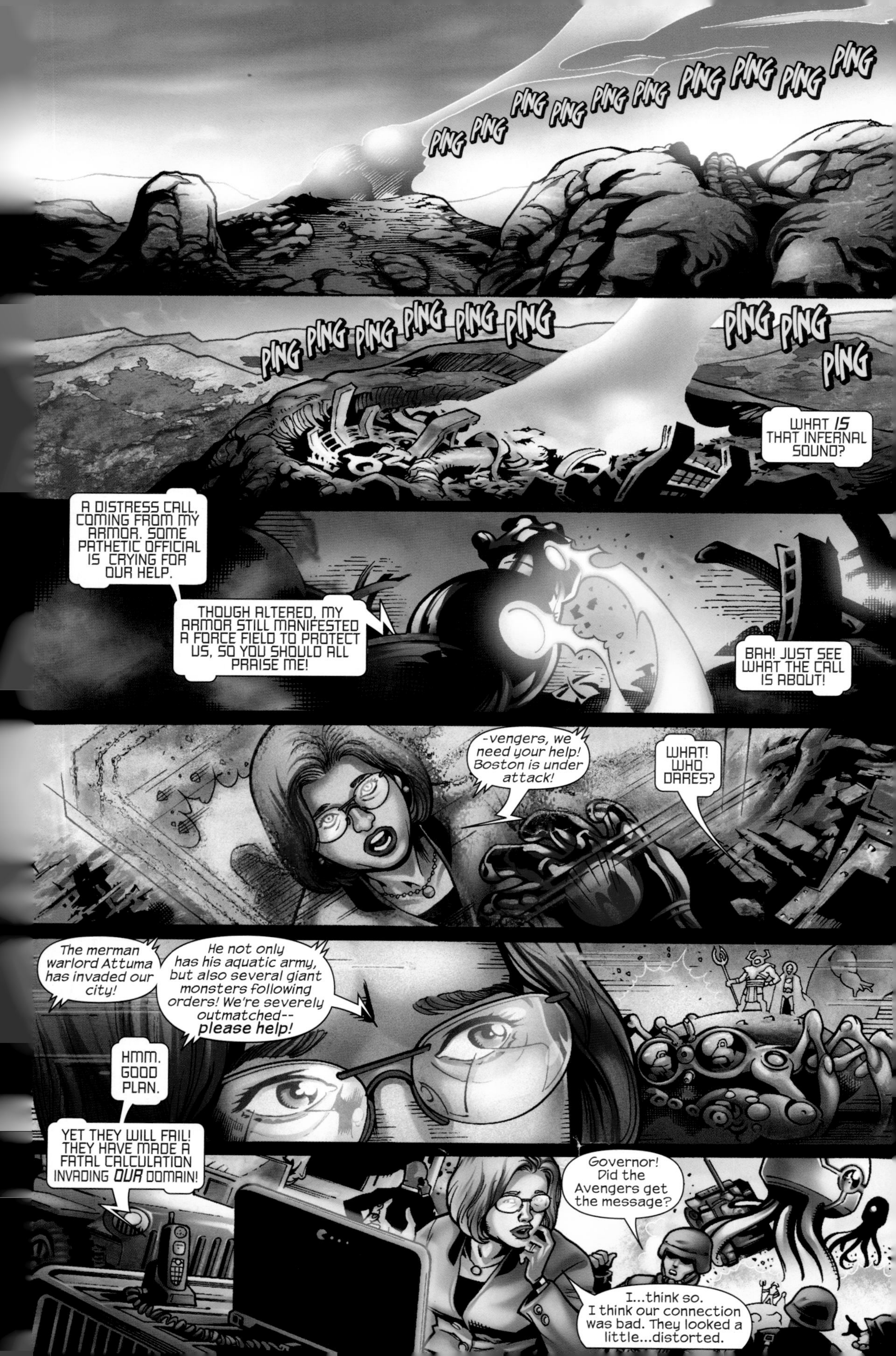
PING PING PING PING PING PING PING PING PING PING
PING PING PING PING PING PING
PING PING PING
WHAT IS THAT INFERNAL SOUND?
A DISTRESS CALL, COMING FROM MY ARMOR. SOME PATHETIC OFFICIAL IS CRYING FOR OUR HELP.
THOUGH ALTERED, MY ARMOR STILL MANIFESTED A FORCE FIELD TO PROTECT US, SO YOU SHOULD ALL PRAISE ME!
BAH! JUST SEE WHAT THE CALL IS ABOUT!
-vengers, we need your help! Boston is under attack!
WHAT! WHO DARES?
The merman warlord Attuma has invaded our city!
He not only has his aquatic army, but also several giant monsters following orders! We're severely outmatched-- please help!
HMM. GOOD PLAN.
YET THEY WILL FAIL! THEY HAVE MADE A FATAL CALCULATION INVADING OUR DOMAIN!
Governor! Did the Avengers get the message?
I...think so. I think our connection was bad. They looked a little...distorted.

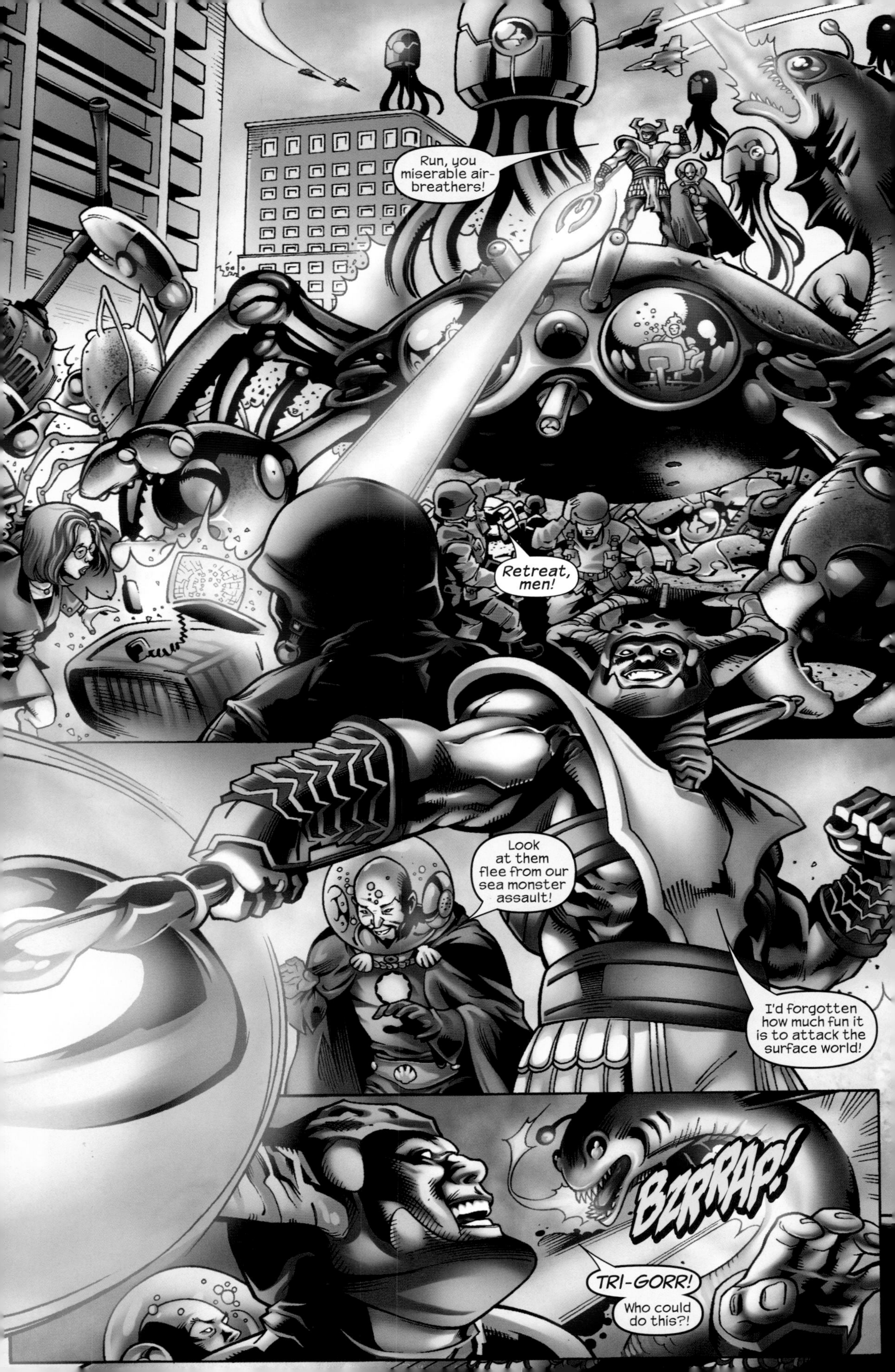

Run, you miserable air-breathers!
Retreat, men!
Look at them flee from our sea monster assault!
I'd forgotten how much fun it is to attack the surface world!
BZRRAP!
TRI-GORR!
Who could do this?!

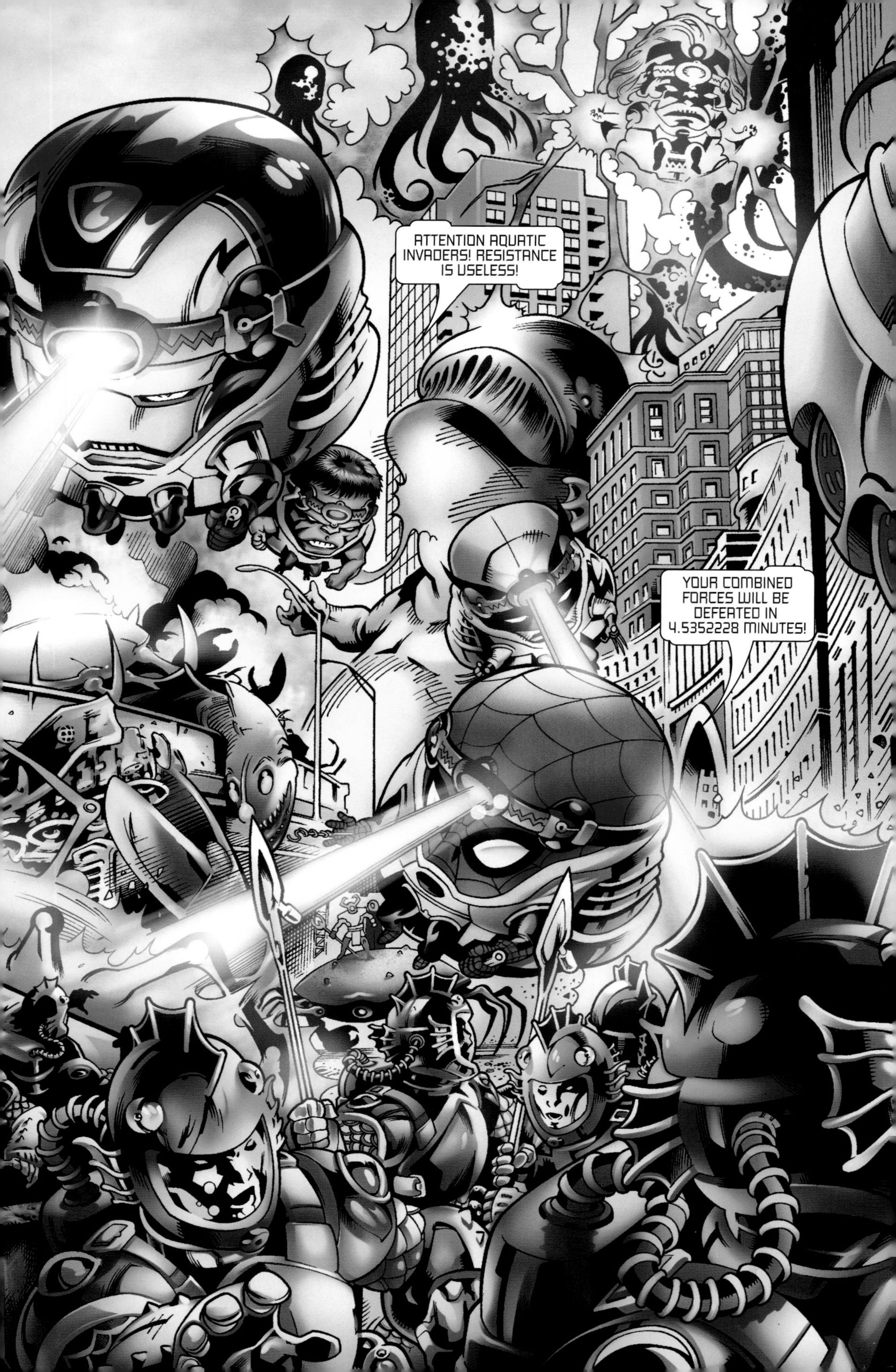
ATTENTION AQUATIC INVADERS! RESISTANCE IS USELESS!
YOUR COMBINED FORCES WILL BE DEFEATED IN 4.5352228 MINUTES!

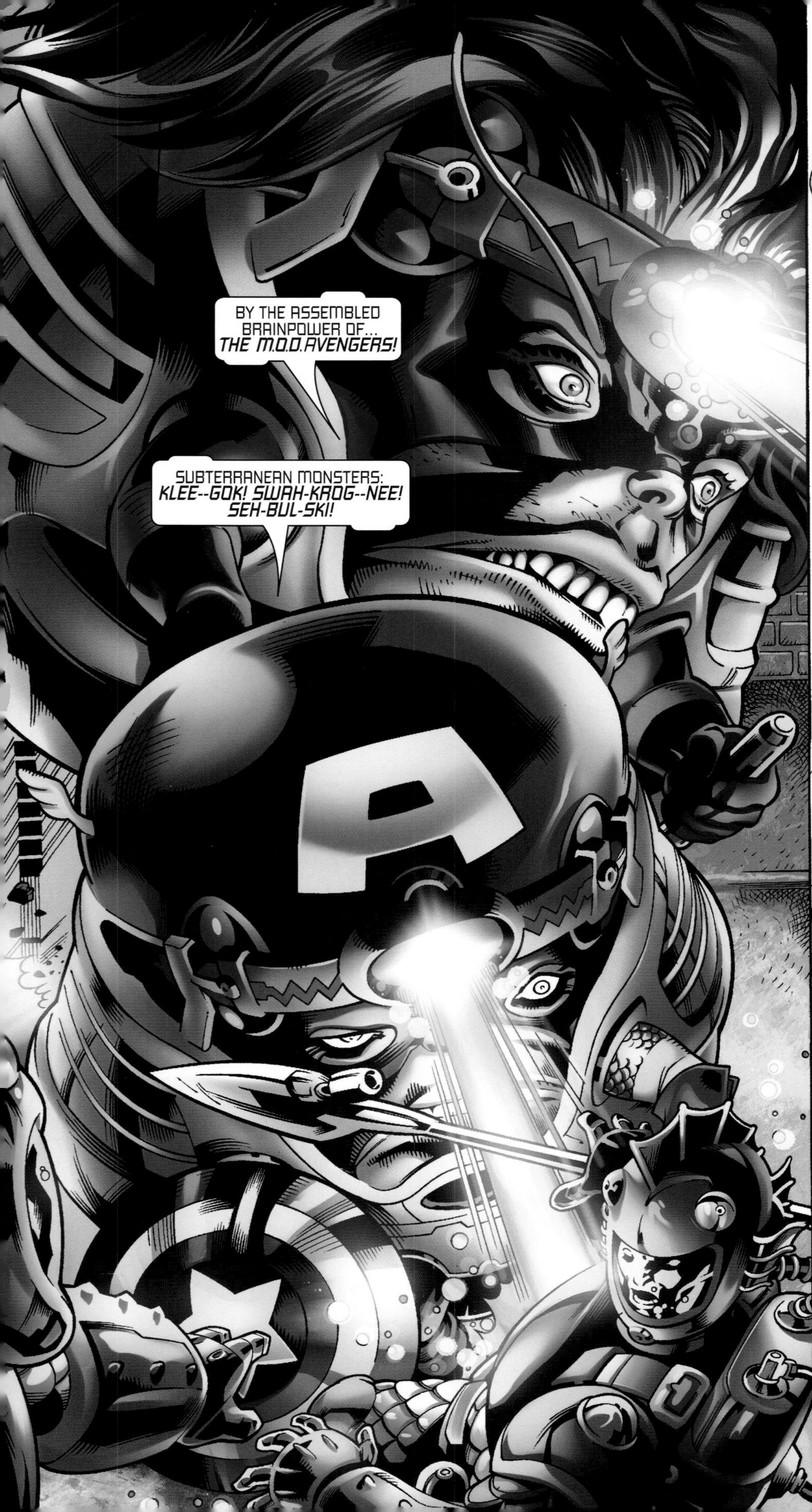
BY THE ASSEMBLED BRAINPOWER OF... THE M.O.D.AVENGERS!
SUBTERRANEAN MONSTERS: KLEE--GOK! SWAH-KROG--NEE! SEH-BUL-SKI!
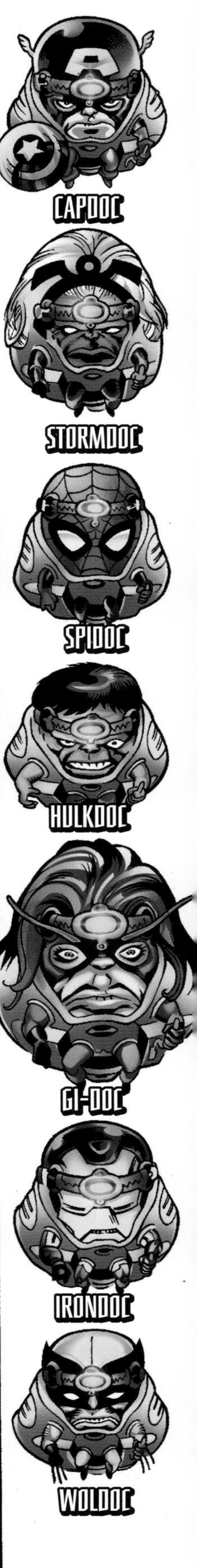
CAPDOC
STORMDOC
SPIDOC
HULKDOC
GI-DOC
IRONDOC
WOLDOC

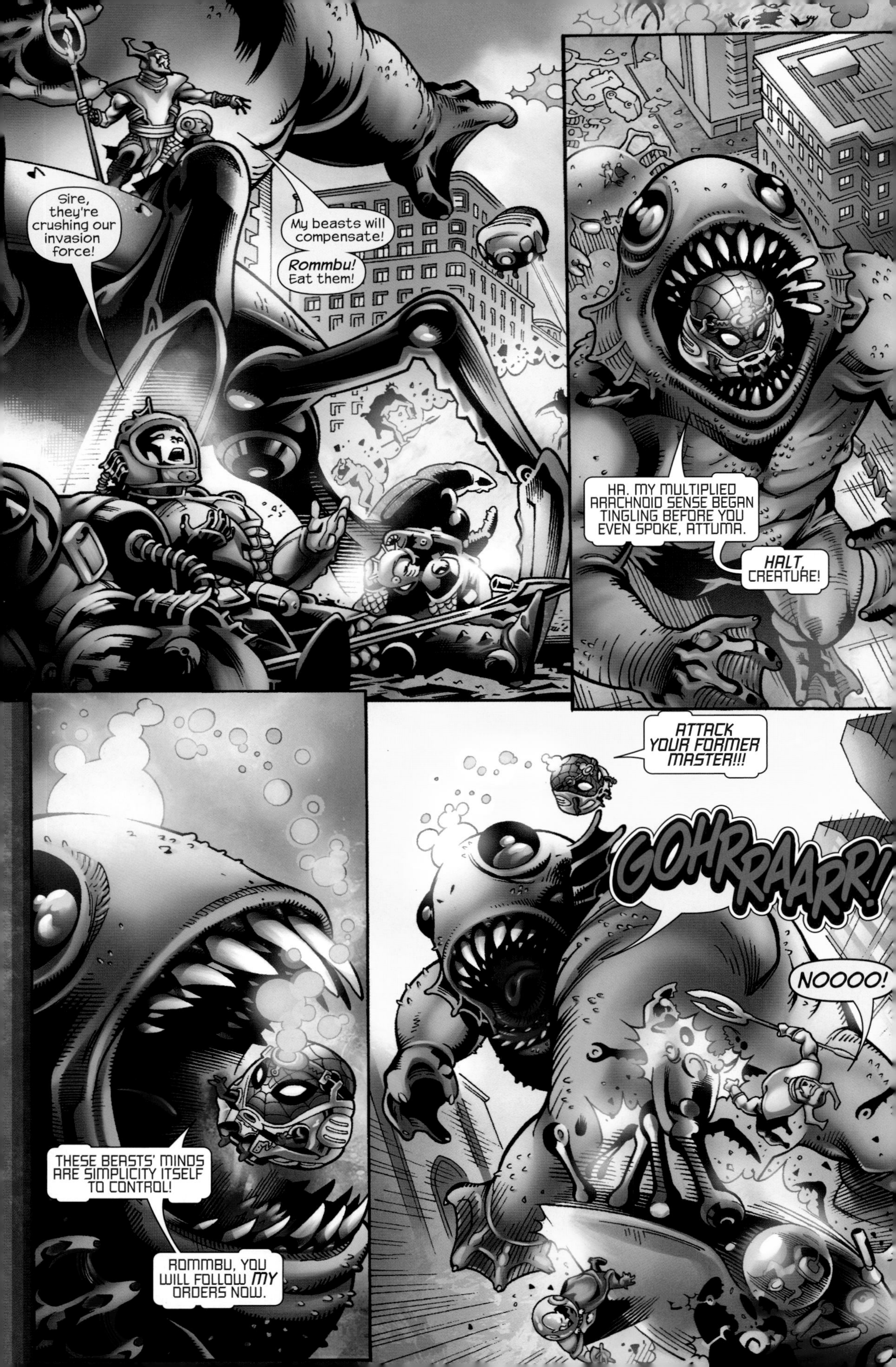
Sire, they're crushing our invasion force!
My beasts will compensate!
Rommbu! Eat them!
HA. MY MULTIPLIED ARACHNOID SENSE BEGAN TINGLING BEFORE YOU EVEN SPOKE, ATTUMA.
HALT, CREATURE!
THESE BEASTS' MINDS ARE SIMPLICITY ITSELF TO CONTROL!
ROMMBU, YOU WILL FOLLOW MY ORDERS NOW.
ATTACK YOUR FORMER MASTER!!!
GOHRRAARR!
NOOOO!

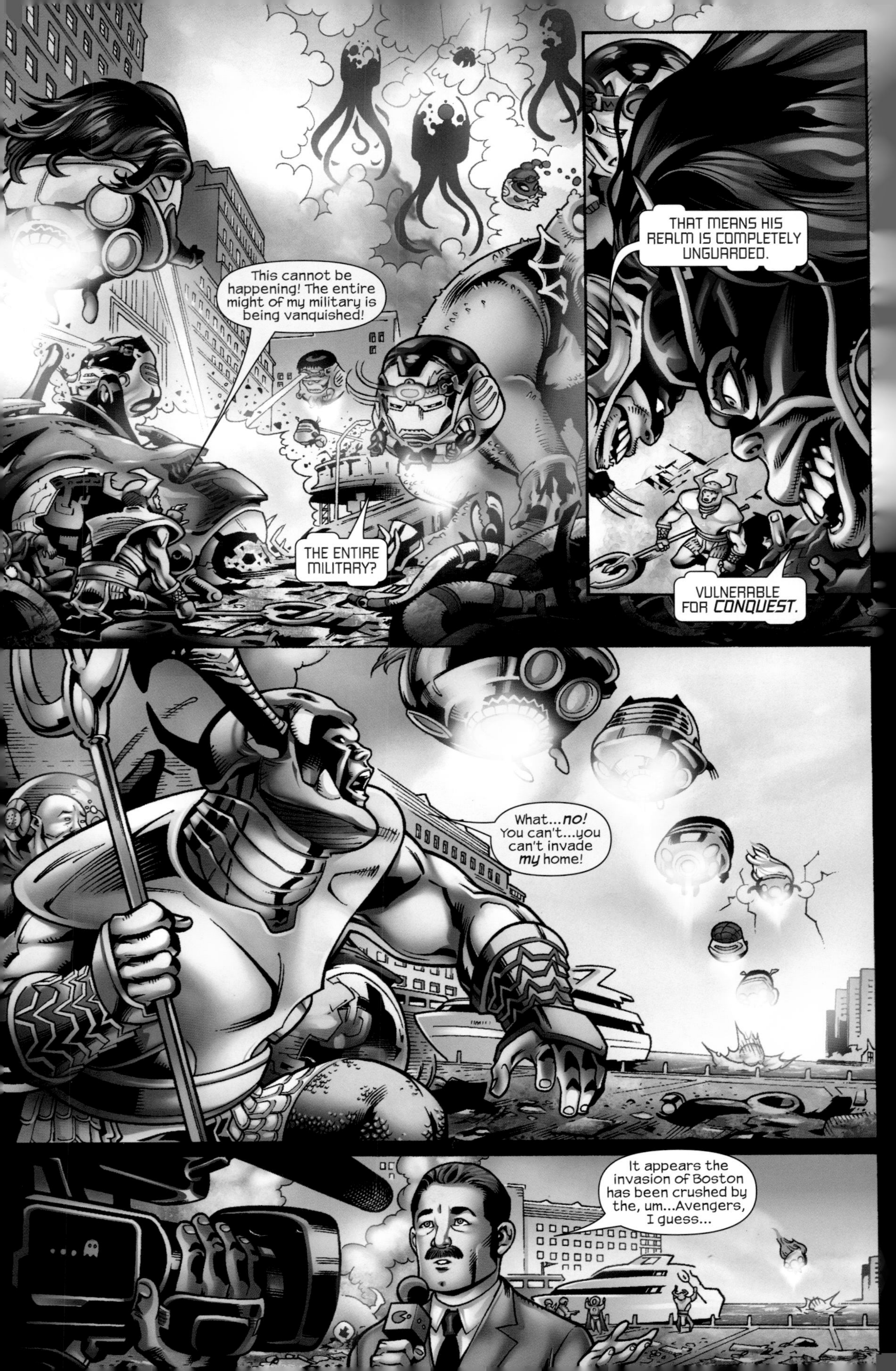
This cannot be happening! The entire might of my military is being vanquished!
THE ENTIRE MILITARY?
THAT MEANS HIS REALM IS COMPLETELY UNGUARDED.
VULNERABLE FOR CONQUEST.
What...no! You can't...you can't invade my home!
It appears the invasion of Boston has been crushed by the, um...Avengers, I guess...

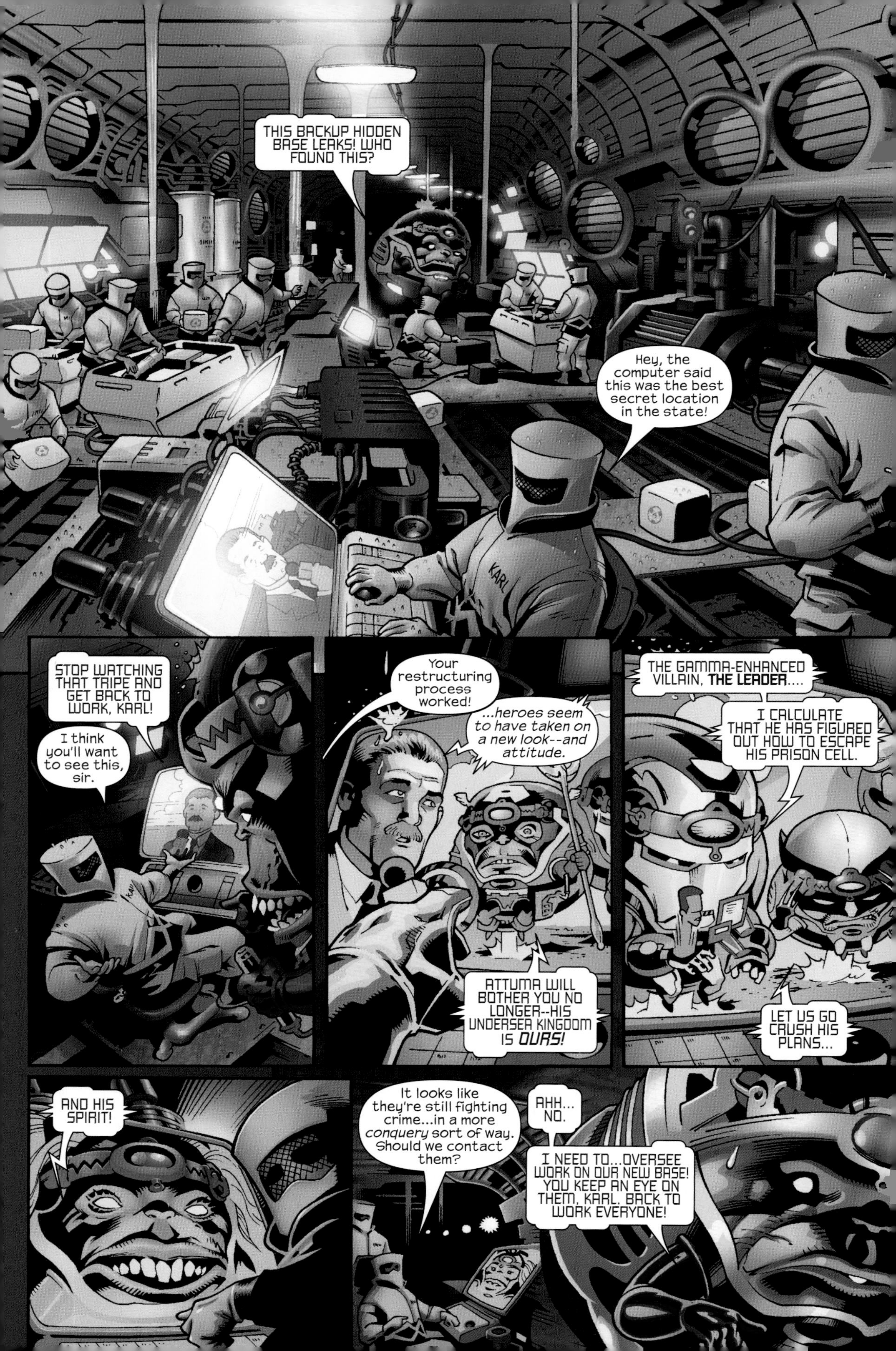
THIS BACKUP HIDDEN BASE LEAKS! WHO FOUND THIS?
Hey, the computer said this was the best secret location in the state!
KARL
STOP WATCHING THAT TRIPE AND GET BACK TO WORK, KARL!
I think you'll want to see this, sir.
Your restructuring process worked!
...heroes seem to have taken on a new look--and attitude.
ATTUMA WILL BOTHER YOU NO LONGER--HIS UNDERSEA KINGDOM IS OURS!
THE GAMMA-ENHANCED VILLAIN, THE LEADER....
I CALCULATE THAT HE HAS FIGURED OUT HOW TO ESCAPE HIS PRISON CELL.
LET US GO CRUSH HIS PLANS...
AND HIS SPIRIT!
It looks like they're still fighting crime...in a more conquery sort of way. Should we contact them?
AHH... NO.
I NEED TO...OVERSEE WORK ON OUR NEW BASE! YOU KEEP AN EYE ON THEM, KARL. BACK TO WORK EVERYONE!

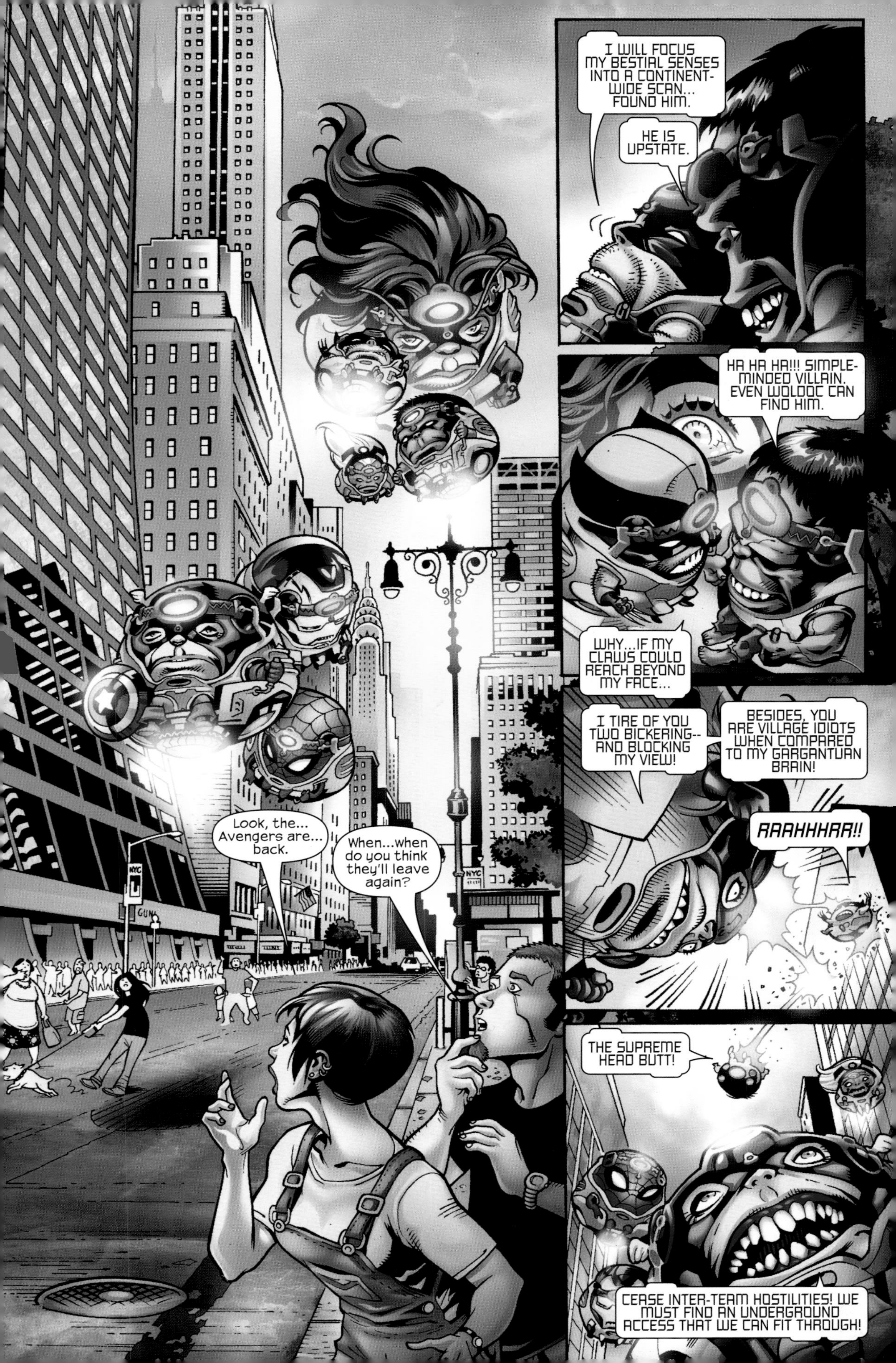
Look, the... Avengers are... back.
When...when do you think they'll leave again?
I WILL FOCUS MY BESTIAL SENSES INTO A CONTINENT-WIDE SCAN... FOUND HIM.
HE IS UPSTATE.
HA HA HA!!! SIMPLE-MINDED VILLAIN. EVEN WOLDOC CAN FIND HIM.
WHY...IF MY CLAWS COULD REACH BEYOND MY FACE...
BESIDES, YOU ARE VILLAGE IDIOTS WHEN COMPARED TO MY GARGANTUAN BRAIN!
I TIRE OF YOU TWO BICKERING-- AND BLOCKING MY VIEW!
AAAHHHAA!!
THE SUPREME HEAD BUTT!
CEASE INTER-TEAM HOSTILITIES! WE MUST FIND AN UNDERGROUND ACCESS THAT WE CAN FIT THROUGH!

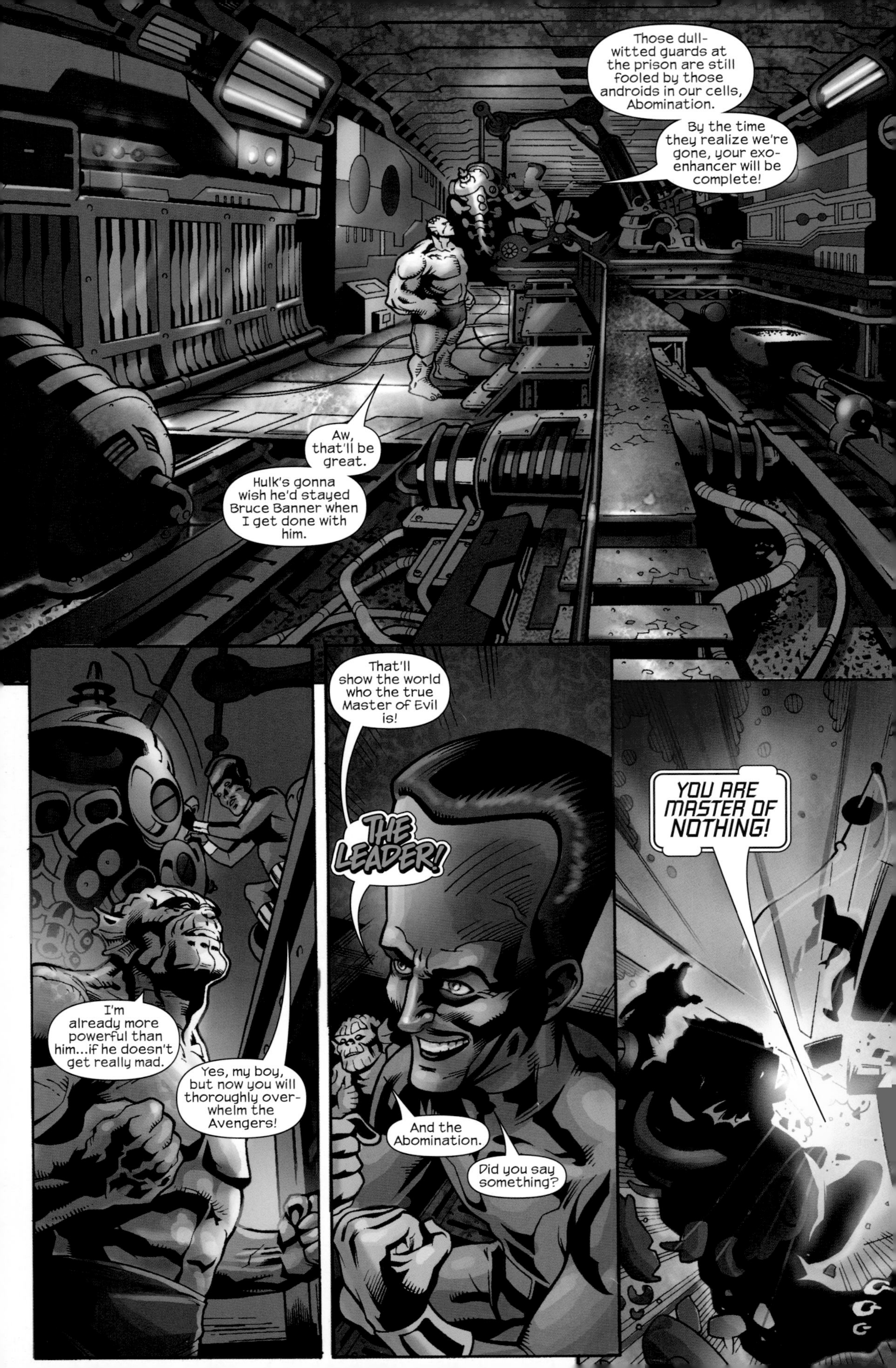
Those dull-witted guards at the prison are still fooled by those androids in our cells, Abomination.
By the time they realize we're gone, your exo-enhancer will be complete!
Aw, that'll be great.
Hulk's gonna wish he'd stayed Bruce Banner when I get done with him.
I'm already more powerful than him...if he doesn't get really mad.
Yes, my boy, but now you will thoroughly over-whelm the Avengers!
That'll show the world who the true Master of Evil is!
THE LEADER!
And the Abomination.
Did you say something?
YOU ARE MASTER OF NOTHING!

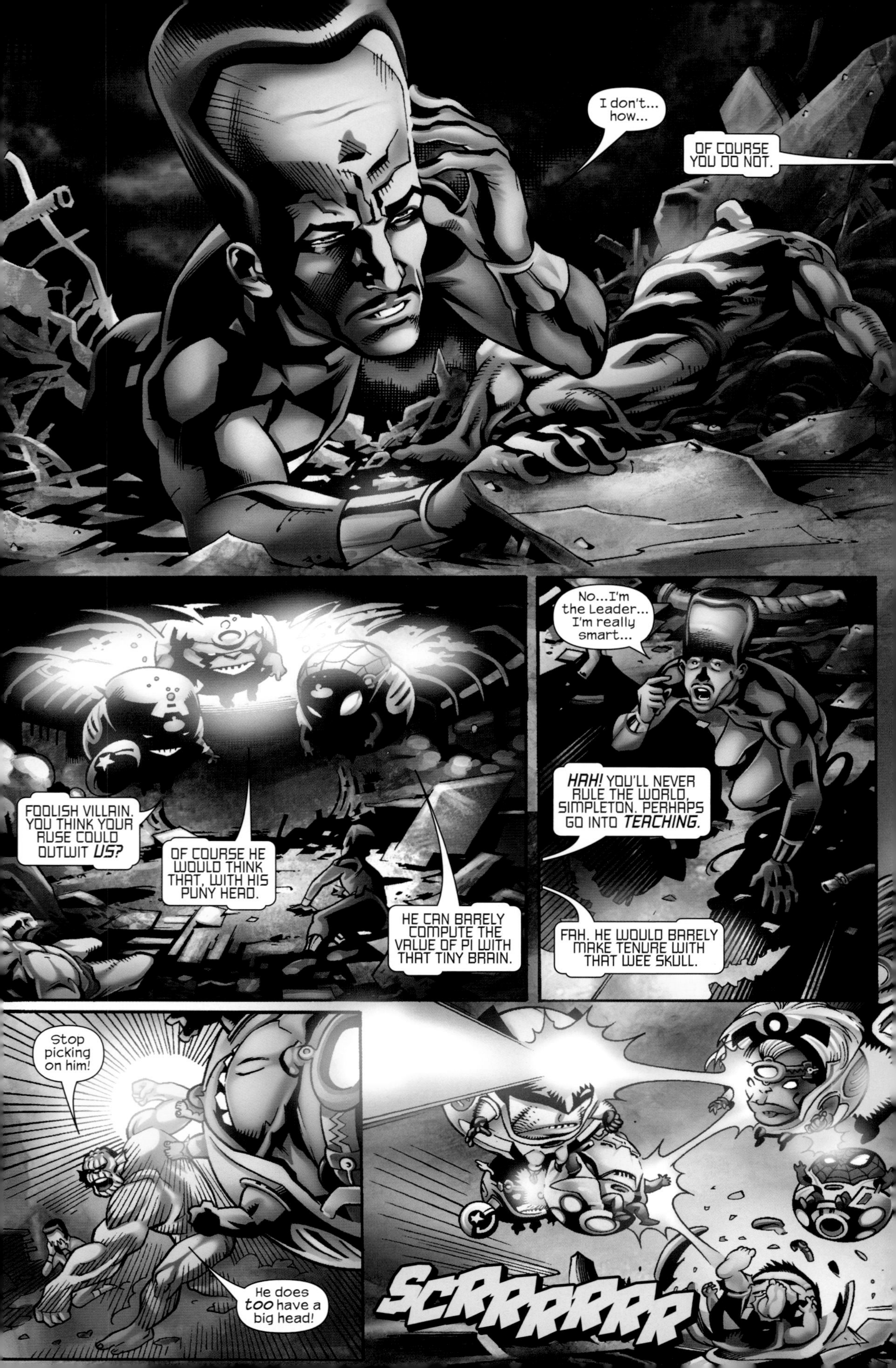
I don't... how...
OF COURSE YOU DO NOT.
FOOLISH VILLAIN. YOU THINK YOUR RUSE COULD OUTWIT US?
OF COURSE HE WOULD THINK THAT, WITH HIS PUNY HEAD.
HE CAN BARELY COMPUTE THE VALUE OF PI WITH THAT TINY BRAIN.
No...I'm the Leader... I'm really smart...
HAH! YOU'LL NEVER RULE THE WORLD, SIMPLETON. PERHAPS GO INTO TEACHING.
FAH. HE WOULD BARELY MAKE TENURE WITH THAT WEE SKULL.
Stop picking on him!
He does too have a big head!
SCRRRRRRR

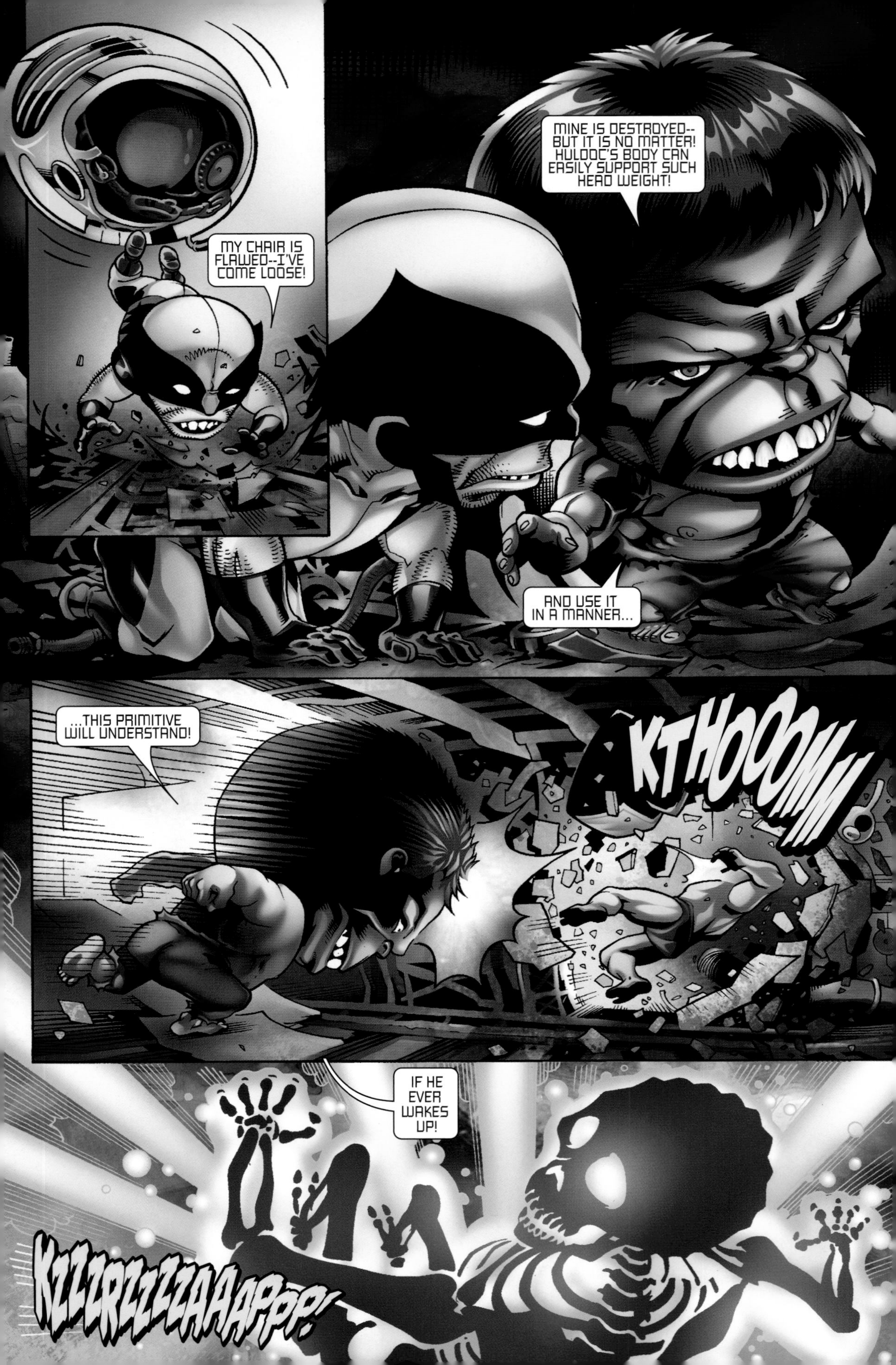
MY CHAIR IS FLAWED--I'VE COME LOOSE!
MINE IS DESTROYED-- BUT IT IS NO MATTER! HULDOC'S BODY CAN EASILY SUPPORT SUCH HEAD WEIGHT!
AND USE IT IN A MANNER...
...THIS PRIMITIVE WILL UNDERSTAND!
KTHOOOMM
IF HE EVER WAKES UP!
KZZZRZZZZAAAPPP!

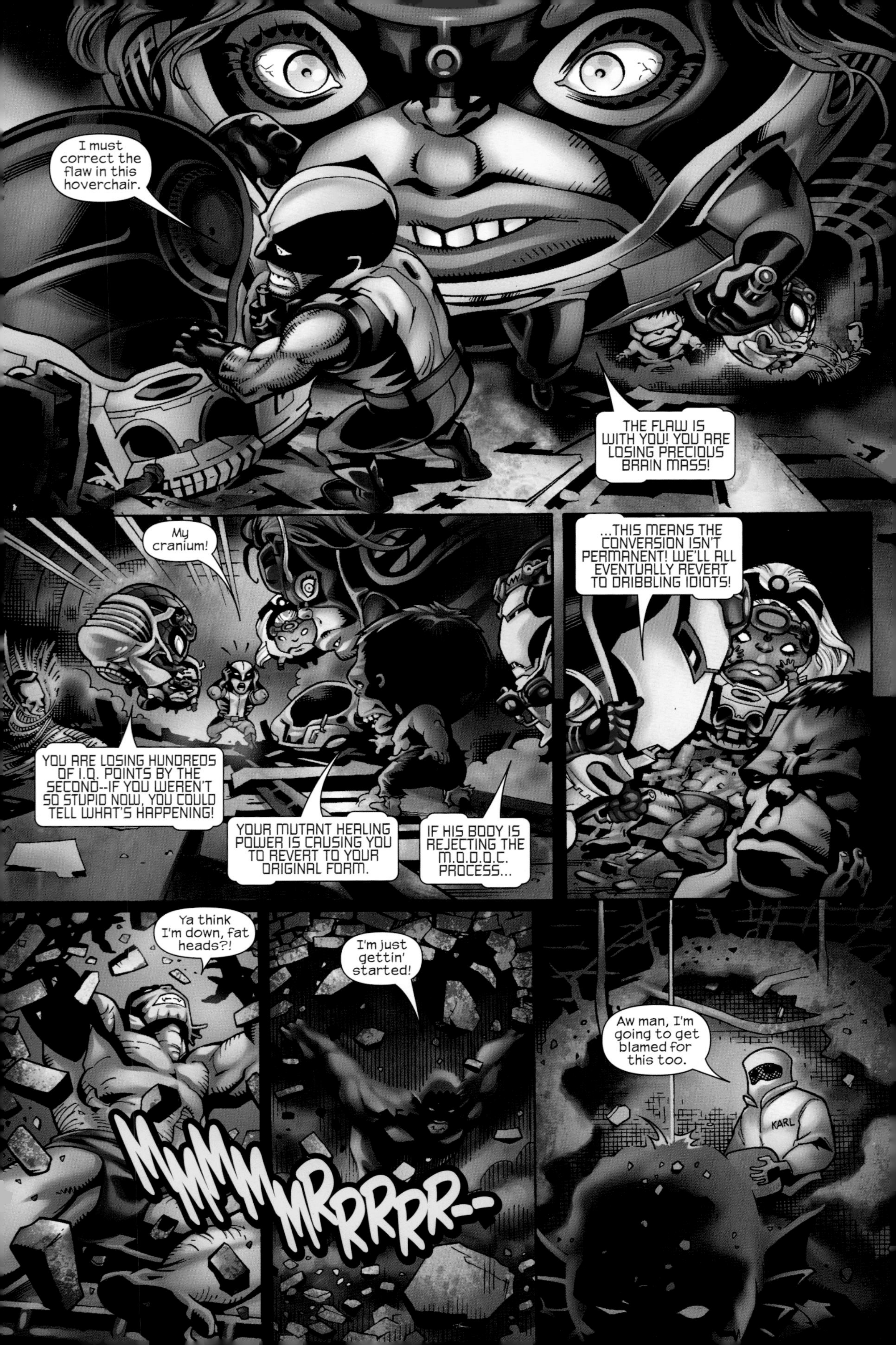
I must correct the flaw in this hoverchair.
THE FLAW IS WITH YOU! YOU ARE LOSING PRECIOUS BRAIN MASS!
My cranium!
YOU ARE LOSING HUNDREDS OF I.Q. POINTS BY THE SECOND--IF YOU WEREN'T SO STUPID NOW, YOU COULD TELL WHAT'S HAPPENING!
YOUR MUTANT HEALING POWER IS CAUSING YOU TO REVERT TO YOUR ORIGINAL FORM.
IF HIS BODY IS REJECTING THE M.O.D.O.C. PROCESS...
...THIS MEANS THE CONVERSION ISN'T PERMANENT! WE'LL ALL EVENTUALLY REVERT TO DRIBBLING IDIOTS!
Ya think I'm down, fat heads?!
I'm just gettin' started!
MMMMMRRRRR--
Aw man, I'm going to get blamed for this too.
KARL

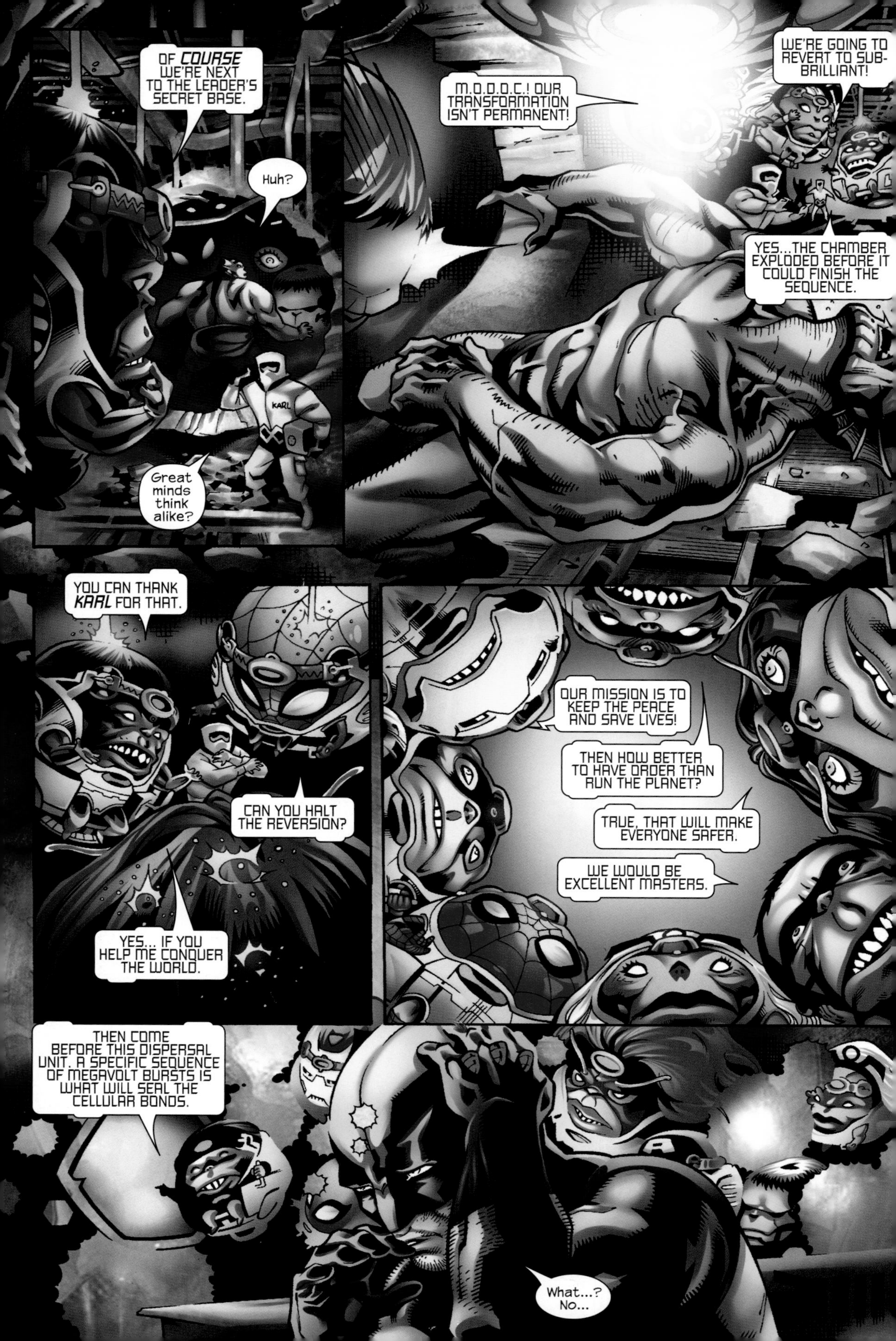
OF COURSE WE'RE NEXT TO THE LEADER'S SECRET BASE.
Huh?
Great minds think alike?
M.O.D.O.C.! OUR TRANSFORMATION ISN'T PERMANENT!
WE'RE GOING TO REVERT TO SUB-BRILLIANT!
YES...THE CHAMBER EXPLODED BEFORE IT COULD FINISH THE SEQUENCE.
YOU CAN THANK KARL FOR THAT.
KARL
CAN YOU HALT THE REVERSION?
YES... IF YOU HELP ME CONQUER THE WORLD.
OUR MISSION IS TO KEEP THE PEACE AND SAVE LIVES!
THEN HOW BETTER TO HAVE ORDER THAN RUN THE PLANET?
TRUE, THAT WILL MAKE EVERYONE SAFER.
WE WOULD BE EXCELLENT MASTERS.
THEN COME BEFORE THIS DISPERSAL UNIT. A SPECIFIC SEQUENCE OF MEGAVOLT BURSTS IS WHAT WILL SEAL THE CELLULAR BONDS.
What...? No...

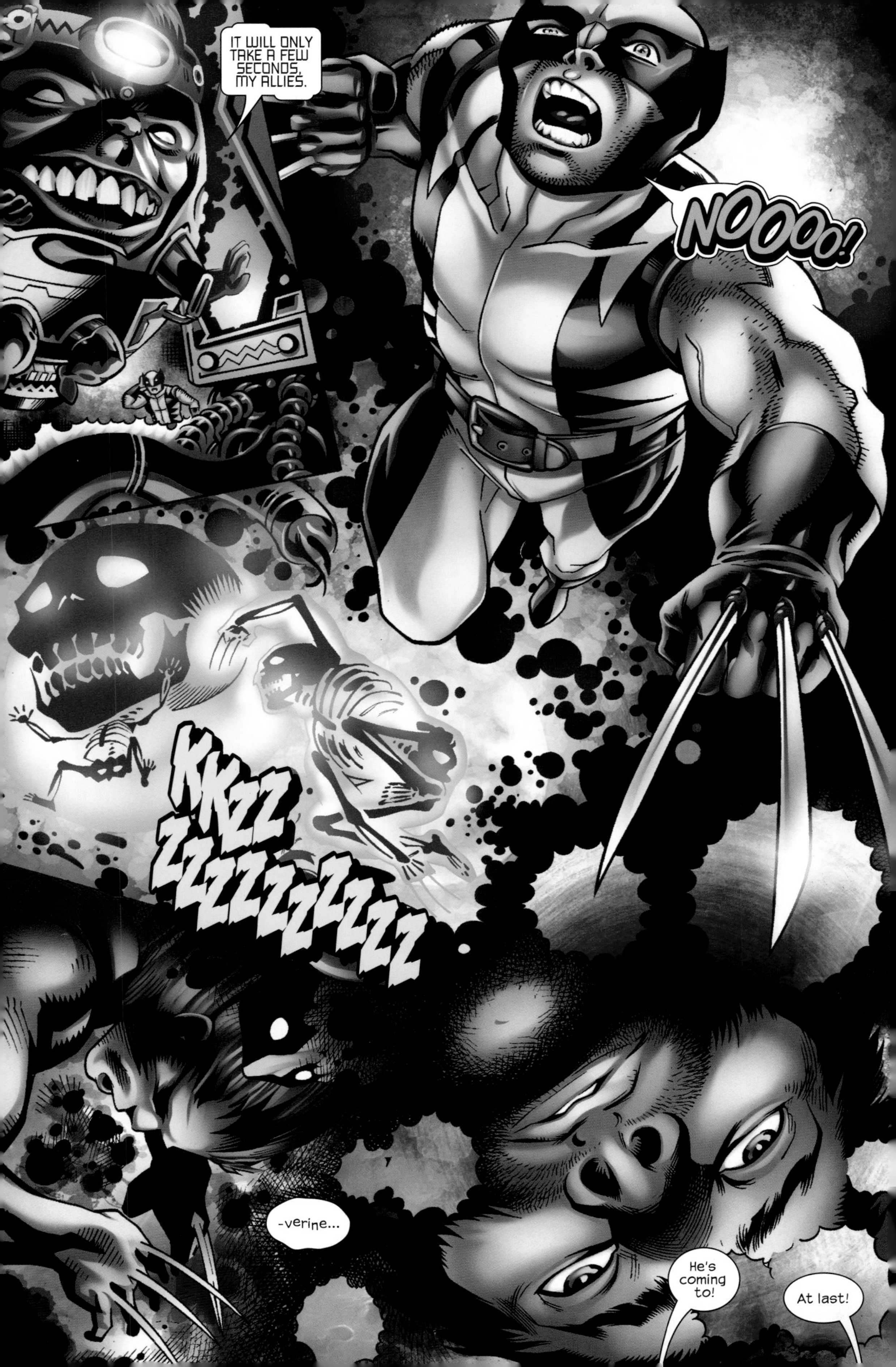
IT WILL ONLY TAKE A FEW SECONDS, MY ALLIES.
NOOOOO!
KKZZZZZZZZZZZZZZZ
-verine...
He's coming to!
At last!

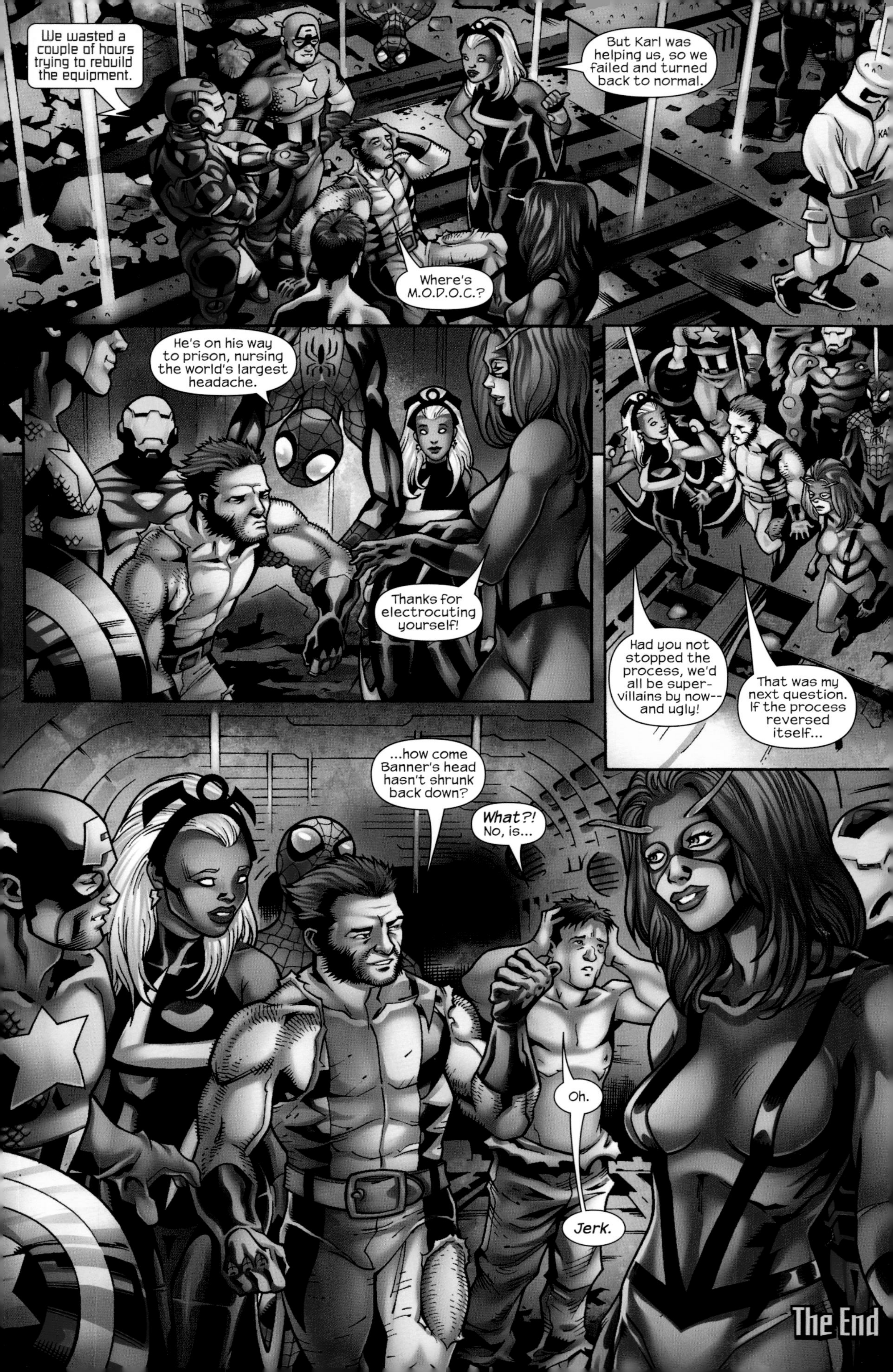
We wasted a couple of hours trying to rebuild the equipment.
But Karl was helping us, so we failed and turned back to normal.
Where's M.O.D.O.C.?
He's on his way to prison, nursing the world's largest headache.
Thanks for electrocuting yourself!
Had you not stopped the process, we'd all be super-villains by now-- and ugly!
That was my next question. If the process reversed itself...
...how come Banner's head hasn't shrunk back down?
What?! No, is...
Oh.
Jerk.
The End